GOODNIGHT BRAMBLE

ROSALYN ROBILLIARD

Published by Water Dragon Publishing
waterdragonpublishing.com

ISBN 978-1-967547-78-4 (Trade Paperback)

FIRST EDITION

10 9 8 7 6 5 4 3 2 1

GOODNIGHT BRAMBLE

F IVE NEW GREY HAIRS. That was the cost. The price to soften the soil. To melt the frost from his grave. Aubree ran her fingers along each wiry thread. Considered plucking them out. But no. She wanted to remember.

"Tea dear?" Lillian pressed a warm mug of something spiced and lemony into Aubree's hands. "Listen, I know it's hard. I've lost a lot of companions along the way. Opal must be my fortieth, maybe even fiftieth owl. But give it another few centuries, you'll learn how to cope." She wedged her round shape next to Aubree on the sofa.

In front of them, smeared plates and lavender cigarettes littered a coffee table, a stack of chocolate wrappers concealing a half-drunk bottle of *Morris Moray's Finest Bourbon*.

"Rip it off like a plaster, I always say," said Saige, kneeling in front of the cold fireplace, blackened matches scattered around her skinny frame. "Get a new one and be done with it. Something short-lived so you don't get too attached. An owl or a hamster. Three or four years is all you get, then *'kccch'*—" She drew a burnt match across her throat.

"*Saige.*" Lillian jerked her head in Aubree's direction.

"*What?*" hissed Saige, losing patience with the matches and sending a bolt of magic from one ashen finger into the grate. Her grey hair loosened from her bun as the room glowed orange in crackling firelight. "You make her feel better then. We're running out of time."

"Aubree, love," Lillian placed a tentative hand on Aubree's knee, "how *are* you getting along with the harvest?"

Aubree grimaced, sinking deeper into her nest of crochet blankets. Her last attempt hadn't gone well. She'd prepared everything as usual: sharpened the knives, put the mice to sleep, counted the newts and rats, bought fresh rags to wipe away the blood. But something was different. It was harder since Bramble had died. He had always been there, rubbing his dark fur across her legs, his deep purr a gentle comfort over the squeals of fear.

"Thought as much," muttered Saige when she didn't reply.

"Oh, my dear," Lillian squeezed Aubree's knee, "I know it's difficult, especially with all that blood. Perhaps we could help?"

"Good idea." Saige stabbed a poker at a burning log,

sparks squealing from its flaming bark. "You can't simply mope around, Aubree. If you won't do it, we will."

"No!" Aubree sat up, almost spilling her tea, conscious of her whiskey-stained dress, of a sweaty, garlicky smell around her neckline. Of the grey in her black hair. Bramble had never judged. He had never expected anything from her. She could almost see him now, curled beside the fire, jade eyes blinking sleepily.

"Well, if you're sure." Saige picked up a pair of bellows, her bony arms pumping furiously until the flames licked up the chimney. "But you know, the market is only two days away."

"Crikey, it's come around quickly hasn't it!" laughed Lillian, her blonde ringlets bobbing around her face. "We've been working so hard I almost lost track of time. *Five* robins Saige managed yesterday and three magpies and two mating pigeons. Songs all bottled and ready! And I picked the ivy and thyme and *even* managed to find some old family recipes for love potions."

"Precisely," said Saige, leaning the bellows beside the now roaring fire. "We simply *cannot* afford to miss selling this month's potions. Lillian and I—" she paused, and Lillian gave her an encouraging smile, "we've put down a deposit on Misty Manor. You know, the big old house at the top of the hill, overlooking the elven forests?"

Aubree nodded vaguely. "Isn't that place haunted?"

"That's the hope," said Lillian. "The ectoplasm would be perfect for our healing elixirs."

"Which is *why*," said Saige, "Aubree, please, we need you to pull yourself together. Hearts of mice are the most important ingredient in a love potion."

Aubree shifted beneath her blanket, the tiny mice twitching and dreaming in her mind, unaware of the butcher's knife raised high above their necks.

"Listen," Lillian lowered her voice, her round face creased in a sad smile, "you know, Bramble was only a cat."

The intended comfort shone clear in her eyes. But the words bit like ice beneath Aubree's skin. She pushed her mug amongst the plates and chocolate wrappers, reaching instead for the whiskey bottle.

"Tomorrow," she said, popping the cork and throwing back a searing swig. "I'll have them for you by noon, at *The Broken Wheel.*"

Saige shot Lillian a look, then picked up her own mug of tea and raised it with an air of finality.

"Tomorrow it is."

Aubree gripped the bottle, stomach already churning. If only she had a pleasant harvest with birdsong and herbs.

•   •   •

That evening, as the moon shone like a chipped coin over snow-capped fir trees, Aubree lit a lantern and crunched through the snow towards the forest. She refused to look at the spot between the vegetable patch and the frozen rope swing. The spot where he now slept forever. She wanted so badly to scoop him up, to cradle him in the folds of her coat, to warm him by the fire.

Her spell drifted over iced leaves, the words melting snow from the rough stone of his grave. Burning hair mingling with pine and chimney smoke as two more black strands fizzed to grey.

The shed sat alone in a clearing; the roof piped in perfect white.

Scurrying and squeaks fled her lantern as she ducked inside, yellow light pooling across the hutches: rats burrowing and kicking; newts shooting like skimming stones into tubs of water; frogs lolloping behind sprays of ivy.

Past the hutches sat a table, a carefully positioned plughole in the centre and a drain beneath. Above, polished knives swayed and creaked on rusty hooks.

Aubree knelt beside the closest hutch, trying not to overthink it. Inside, a mouse peeked out from a hollow log, its fur russet brown like autumn leaves. She held the lantern up to see more clearly, then with her other hand, pressed her fingers to the wire mesh.

Sleep

A simple command. The magic barely perceptible as it slipped from her body, two tiny eyelashes fizzing and loosening onto her cheek. Nothing like a death spell. One spark of that and she'd be a withered prune, if even alive.

The mouse blinked then curled into a ball, tail tucked beneath its whiskered chin. Aubree unlatched the hutch and shuffled the sleeping animal into her palm, its warm breath tickling her fingers.

The mice weren't so bad really. They could sleep through it all, dreaming as lovers did. Their hearts taken before they knew what was happening. The rats were worse though. She would need to take their tails awake—capture the fear and adrenaline of love.

She laid the mouse on the table beside the lantern, a shadow cradling protectively around it. Her own dark eyes stared back from the blade of the butcher's knife as she unhooked it from the wall.

Whiskers twitched with a dream, pink nose sniffing under tightly closed eyes. Bramble had dreamed like that. Perhaps catching dream-mice like this one. She paused. She had to be strong. He was only a cat. He was only a cat. He was only a cat.

Her hand shook as she brought down the knife, the blade landing with a heavy 'thud'. A drop of condensation splattered from the ceiling and a creature rustled in the straw behind her.

She looked down at the tiny shape, still sleeping unharmed, the knife burrowed deep into the tabletop. What kind of a witch was she? But worse, how had she ever done this before? Her throat burned with the aftertaste of whiskey and she grappled for the lantern, stumbling back towards the door.

The outside privy sat dark and alone at the edge of the forest. She ran towards it, hand clamped over her mouth, only just making it in time. Tears streamed down her cheeks as she knelt over the toilet, stomach emptying.

Pathetic. She leaned back against the rough timber wall, wiping her mouth with a scrap of newspaper. If only Bramble was here, one touch of his black fur, one nudge of his nose, it would all feel easier, better. But he wasn't, was he? And whose fault was that?

She clenched her frozen toes in her boots, feeling the pain. She deserved this. She had let Bramble down.

"Useless," she whispered. "What kind of a witch ..."

Her gaze fell on the crumpled newspaper, still clutched in her stiff fingers.

'*Tired of all the killing? Want to feel revitalised?*'

She smoothed out the scrap on her knees.

Tired of all the killing? Want to feel revitalised? Join the No Death Society, every week at the deep caverns. A group of like-minded trolls sharing human-free recipes, support with killing less and good conversation! Plus, special guest Gideon the Good will do a talk on his new book: 'From Carnage to Cabbage: My journey with the No Death Movement'.

Aubree frowned and re-read the advert. She *was* tired of all the killing. She *did* want to feel revitalised. The next meeting was tomorrow. Trolls couldn't do magic. But perhaps they might understand how she was feeling, unlike Saige and Lillian.

She glanced over the advert once more then stood, stuffing it into her pocket. If she was really going to commit to this, there was one thing she needed to do first.

• • •

The next day, shortly before noon, Aubree winced at her table in *The Broken Wheel* as she heard the distant roar of a flame-thrower spell. A moment later, Saige kicked open the door, mink hat dripping with melted snow.

"Ohh, it's cosy in here," cooed Lillian behind her, unwrapping her scarf and shaking snow from her boots.

"Port! And a wheel of your finest Stilton," barked

Saige, marching past the wilting barman and snatching a chair from a neighbouring table.

"Morning, Aubree!" Saige slammed the chair down ferociously. "Goodness! You look awful!"

Aubree groaned and buried her head in her hands.

"Been a long night."

Saige glanced at Lillian with a satisfied smile. "Does this mean the harvest was successful?"

"Yes," pressed Lillian, "are the jars all at your house?" She poured a fresh flask of turmeric tea into a tankard. "We made a start on heating the robin song this morning, it's coming along beautifully."

"NO NOT THAT," snapped Saige as the serving boy handed her a board with a large round of gooey cheese. "Are you blind? This is Camembert! Stilton, I said STIL-TON!" The boy hurried back behind the bar, almost dropping the cheese.

Aubree lit a fresh lavender cigarette, trying to stop her hands from shaking.

"So, where have you put them?" Saige peered beneath the table.

Aubree inhaled deeply, unable to meet their eyes. "I set them all free," she whispered in a puff of lavender smoke.

The fire crackled and the serving boy returned, grinning triumphantly with a board of Stilton and a crystal cut glass of port. With one glance at their faces his smile vanished. He hurried to wedge the food between them, shaking so badly that he sloshed Lillian's tea all over her skirt.

"HOW DARE YOU?" roared Saige, launching to her feet and sending a furious bolt of magic at the boy. With a pop, a small, flapping bat appeared in his place. At the same time,

Saige's hair exploded from its grey bun, sending hairpins flying across the tavern. The other villagers hastily downed their drinks and made a beeline for the frozen wasteland outside.

"Oh Saige! There was no need for that!" Lillian scooped the terrified bat into her palms.

But Saige wasn't listening. She rounded on Aubree. "YOU SET THEM FREE? I'm sorry, but I have had ENOUGH, Aubree. We have been patient, beyond patient. But you have to *see!* We need this money. Who knows when a place like Misty Manor will come up again."

"It's not what it sounds like," said Aubree quickly. "I'm going to ask the No Death Society for help."

There was a pause, in which Lillian tried to feed a conciliatory piece of Stilton to the bat.

"What," hissed Saige, "in the name of sweet magic, is the *No Death Society*?"

"It's a sort of ... club, for trolls who don't want to eat humans anymore. It means no more killing. It means the animals get to live—all of them, I mean."

Saige pursed her lips. "But what are we supposed to put in our potions?"

"We'll work it out! I'm going to my first meeting this afternoon."

"Aubree." Saige spoke with the kind of forced low voice that suggested she was holding back a great deal of anger. "*Trolls can't do magic.*"

"I don't see what that has to do with it. There's no need to be prejudiced."

"You're asking for their advice *on magic!* You might as well ask that bloody serving boy what he thinks!"

"Well maybe I could have, if you hadn't turned him into a bat."

"That's beside the point! We're talking about the potions *you* agreed to make—"

"Oh yes, I forgot, all you care about is making money."

There was a silence. Saige seething, Lillian prodding motherly at the bat, Aubree tapping ash furiously from her cigarette.

"No," said Saige. "I care about *people*. Living, breathing people who need me. Not a–a–", she shook her head. "You know what, Aubree? You go to your blasted troll meeting. *We*," she pointed a furious finger at Lillian, "are going to do proper witch's work!" She stomped across the tavern, wrestled her fur coat from the hatstand and slammed the door behind her.

Lillian looked at Aubree, her mouth falling open as if to say something. Then she sighed and shook her head.

"I'm sorry, Aubree, but Saige is right." She rummaged in her dress pocket then slid a scrap of paper over the table. "Farmer Wilderspin's advertising a litter of silver foxes. The sooner you move on, the sooner you'll be happy. And we can all get back to normal."

She tickled the bat on the head. "Don't worry, it'll wear off soon."

Aubree sat for a while, lavender cigarette burning low, staring at the advertisement, then in one swift movement she scrunched it into a ball.

What had she been thinking? Setting the animals free. Perhaps the whiskey had gone to her head. But she just couldn't *bear* the thought of ... she shuddered and took another long drag. Either way the animals were gone. Whether Saige and Lillian liked it or not, the trolls were their only hope.

•   •   •

It was a steep, rocky hike from *The Broken Wheel* to the deep caverns, so Aubree hired a horse from the landlady.

"You tell Saige, I want compensation," grumbled the skinny old woman as Aubree hoisted herself into the saddle. "I lost good business over that bat stunt. And don't go doing anything witchy to Marbles!" she called as Aubree kicked the horse's flank.

He was a good horse, a sturdy chestnut, but the flint paths were black with ice, and she found herself slowing him so often that she was almost fifteen minutes late by the time she reached the jagged tear in the side of the mountain.

The cavern beyond glowed orange with the distant light of a fire and a deep rumble echoed through the caves, tinkling the icy stalactites around the entrance.

Aubree tied Marbles to a whitened fir tree, melting snow in a bowl for him to drink.

"I'll be back soon." She ruffled his hazel fringe, then crept into the cave, her boots slipping on the ice. After a while, the echoes turned into words.

"Now *this* is something special. Hey, come now! Give it a chance."

Aubree edged around the corner, peering into a vast cavern below where four trolls squatted next to a fire, the largest pumpkin she had ever seen swollen and bubbling on a spit. The trolls were all about twice the height of an average human, their skin varying shades of tarnished silver, glinting under the firelight, and mottled with scars. And they were all staring with rapt attention at a willowy and glamorous ... witch?

Aubree sucked in her breath. There was another witch here. Her hair shone white, coiffed into an elegant bob, and she was rummaging in an enormous, coral pink suitcase. After a moment, she re-emerged brandishing what appeared to be a beige hot dog.

"And if you like these boys, I've plenty more where they came from," she drawled. "I've got sandals made from finest death-free leather, and a gen-u-ine, one of a kind, never before seen *piece of death-free cheese,* also egg that ain't never seen a chicken and the very finest alternatives to bacon, sausages, quiche, mince ..."

"We don't eat none of that," grunted the largest troll. "Oi, Gideon, who is this? We came to see you speak, not her."

"Vanessa Velentuia, finest death-free alternatives." She pushed a card into the troll's huge hand. "And not just food alternatives, oh no! I see you're wearing leather. Is that human skin or pig?"

"Er, a mix?" said the troll, adjusting his tunic self-consciously. "It was me dad's, so I didn't think it mattered? I didn't buy it," he added.

"Ah, no no no, I don't mean to *criticise,* I'm sure your dad was the height of fashion—1700s, was it? Very interesting era. But you've got to think about the *image.* You can't wander around lecturing people on not killing humans with a string of ears around your neck. Now this!" She rummaged again in her suitcase, and produced a small black cap. "Take a look at *this*." She pushed the cap into the troll's hand. It barely covered the end of his finger.

"What is it?"

"Oh, it's just a sample. But look at the fabric. Would you believe me if I told you that it's made ONE HUNDRED PERCENT from plants? *(andalsosomeadditiveswhichmay ormaynotincludethoseofmagicaloriginandmayormayno tcauseyouharm)*"

"What?"

"Never mind, take a look at these pictures." She produced a handful of glossy brochures. Aubree peered closer and saw what looked like muscular trolls posing in tight leather outfits and ... she squinted further ... they were holding various vegetables. Carrots, onions ... she felt herself blush.

"Cor," muttered the troll. "Gideon, look at them!"

"Shall I sign you up for two outfits each? Of course, it depends whether you want our basic package, or the supreme. The basic includes one chest harness, two sets of shorts and a pair of boots. But with the supreme package, you get the chest harness, shorts, boots AND gloves, a 20% off code for your next purchase and a free pen."

"Erm," said Gideon uncertainly.

It was at this point that one of Aubree's feet finally surrendered to the ice, sliding into a stone which clattered and scraped down the slope towards the figures huddled around the fire.

"Who's that?" shouted Gideon.

"It came from over there!" cried a squat troll, his face covered in pockmarks and lumps.

"Er, hello," said Aubree, picking her way down the slope and into the firelight.

"A *human*," hissed the squat troll.

"No, I don't think so," murmured Vanessa, eyes narrowing. "That's a witch."

"Yes," said Aubree, trying to stand a little straighter, "and I'd like to join your erm ... club."

"Easy now," rumbled Gideon to his fellow trolls. "I'll handle this." He turned towards Aubree and Vanessa. "Now I don't know how you've ended up here."

"I saw your advert," said Aubree, digging out the newspaper scrap and holding it up.

"Eh?" the troll peered at the advert. "Oh, bloody hell, Keith." He glowered at the squat troll, who had helped himself to a slab of pumpkin. "How do you explain this?"

"You said we needed to reach a new audience." Keith shrugged.

"A new audience! Keith, not *humans*, not *witches*. What are we going to do having them coming to our meetings? 'Come along Mr. and Mrs. Troll, we'll help you stop eating humans, oh by the way WE'LL HAVE SOME TO TEMPT YOU ALONG THE WAY!'"

Several stalactites fell from the ceiling and Keith chewed sloppily on his pumpkin slice.

"Why have you come here anyway?" grumbled Gideon. "Witches don't eat humans. Do you?"

Vanessa shrugged. "Not anymore. But as you can see, I'm not with *her.*" She glowered at Aubree. "What are *you* doing here? I didn't know there were other witches selling death-free wares in these parts."

"I—," Aubree felt quite stupid now she was standing

in front of them all. "I came for advice. I wanted to ..." then an idea struck her. Trolls couldn't do magic. But Vanessa could. "Have you ever made ... well I guess you'd call it ... a *death-free potion*?"

Vanessa inspected her for a moment, seeming to consider whether this might be some sort of trick.

"You got gold?" she asked, eyes narrowing.

Aubree rooted around in her pocket and produced a handful of coins. Vanessa smiled, a broad grin of polished white teeth.

"Listen boys," she turned to the trolls, "the witchling and I are taking a little stroll. I'll leave you with these," she handed out more of her glossy brochures, "then we can wrap up a few orders when I'm back, okay lovelies?"

The trolls glared at her.

"Come on sweetie." She clicked her fingers, the suitcase folding up into a pink clutch bag which she slung over one wrist, then beckoned for Aubree to follow her deeper into the caverns.

"Where are we going?" Aubree pulled out a box of matches, striking a flame to light their way. Vanessa ignored her.

"Do you know how I sell so many death-free products? I'll tell you," she said, before Aubree could reply. "*Feeling.* If there's one thing death-free leather has that real leather just can't contend with, it's *feeling.* And I don't mean the softness of the leather. Oh no. I mean how it *feels* to wear something guilt free. It's liberating. *Revitalising.* I don't need to sell them. They sell themselves. Ah, here we go."

They ducked into a low cave, the ceiling dripping in twisted stalactites, Aubree's match the only light.

"So, you want a death-free potion? No nasty rat's tails? No gruesome newt's eyes or hearts of mice? Guilt free?"

Aubree felt a flicker of nerves. Was it really a good idea to follow a strange witch into the deep caverns for experimental magic? But if Vanessa really could brew a death-free potion, she might never have to make another harvest.

"Well, I should warn you, they're not like normal potions. You can't just decide you want a love potion and then 'poof' there's a love potion. You get what you get." Vanessa winked, then clicked her fingers again, the suitcase popping back onto the floor. She laid out several jars of herbs and flowers, lit an oil lantern and propped a cast-iron cauldron to bubble over a blue flame.

"Now," she began unscrewing lids, the fire crackling and spitting behind her, "the reason rat's tails work so well is because they are filled to the tip with fear. The eyes of newts see deep into their futures, longing for what they cannot have. Hearts of mice skip and dream, in love with a world free from predators. They're all feelings, Aubree, darling. Just like those you and I have."

Without warning, she lifted a handful of Aubree's hair and buried her nose between the black strands, inhaling deeply. Aubree pulled away in alarm.

"You smell like *feeling* to me, dear. Strong too. Quickly now, sit down, cross-legged, that's right, close your eyes."

Aubree reluctantly shut her eyes, the dark swirl of her inner eyelids popping in flashes and streaks of colour.

"Now, it's quite simple. You just need to *feel*. Exactly like the mice do. We need to collect your *love*."

Aubree's eyes snapped open. "My *love*?" She let out an embarrassed laugh. "I'm not feeling love."

"Yes, you are, sweetie, I can smell it a mile off."

Aubree glanced at her own black hair doubtfully. "You must be smelling somebody else." Love was the last thing she was feeling. Pain, yes. Guilt, yes. Stupid, yes, yes, yes.

Vanessa smiled, then inhaled again, her eyes flickering shut. "Let's see … musty fur and a sleepy yawn of cat grass and … oh my, fish biscuits!" She laughed. "Love sweetie, it smells different for everyone, but it's as plain as day on you."

Aubree shifted uncomfortably. "But what about the guilt, the regret? Can't you smell that?"

"And how would that smell, my darling?"

Aubree thought of Bramble. Of his jade eyes and rumbling purr. Of his kneading paws and soft, black fur. Of his fishy yawns. She laughed, her breath catching. Tears filled her eyes. She loved him. She loved him so much.

"That's it, dear," murmured Vanessa.

Was that the reason it hurt so badly? Why she felt that terrible burning guilt? That awful regret? Was it all just because she loved him so much?

"Ow!" Aubree fell backwards as Vanessa plucked out a hair.

"Got it!" She threw the hair into the cauldron with a handful of flowers and herbs.

Aubree leaned forwards, watching the black strand sparking and fizzing in the mixture, the scent of cat grass and fish biscuits curling in the steam. It smelt like Bramble. Did that mean it really was love she was feeling? A strange sense of relief and embarrassment washed over her. *He was only a cat.*

Was it okay that she loved him so much? Saige and Lillian would say she needed to pull herself together. The potion bubbled and puffed out another comforting waft. Maybe they were wrong.

•　　•　　•

An hour later, Aubree reluctantly emptied her pockets of far too much gold in exchange for a small box of bottled potions. Vanessa looked so pleased she didn't even complain when the trolls only ordered one death-free leather chest harness.

"I'd say come again, but best not to," grumbled Gideon, as Aubree climbed into Marbles' saddle. "My parents are giving it a go next week and I'm thinking I'll ease them into it with a switch to horsemeat." He eyed Marbles and Aubree laughed uneasily.

"See you around, Aubree." Vanessa winked, counting her new riches with a glint in her eye.

•　　•　　•

It was dark by the time Aubree reached Saige and Lillian's house; the little crooked building lodged around the trunk of a sprawling oak tree. The smell of toasted herbs rose from the chimney as a thin plume of smoke curled into the starry sky. Aubree could hear chattering inside, the leaded windows clouded with condensation, soft jazz drifting into the night.

She felt for the cool glass of the death-free potion wedged snugly in her pocket, then rapped loudly on the front door. "Lillian! Saige? It's Aubree!" She couldn't wait to see Saige's face when she saw the death-free potion.

Feet scrabbled behind the door and the jazz crackled to silence.

"Erm, just coming, dear!" Lillian pulled open the door, her cheeks flushed and rosy, ringlets frizzy with steam. "Aubree, thank goodness you're alright." She pulled Aubree into a tight hug.

"I'm more than alright," Aubree stepped back, "you'll never guess what I've got!"

"Got dear? Erm, what have you got?"

"I'll tell you both! Saige?" Aubree squeezed past her. "I went to see the trolls and we made a death-free potion—" She stopped, halfway through the door.

The air hung thick, smoky. Herbs drooped from the ceiling, pastel cushioned benches soft and inviting. In the centre of the room, beneath the towering tree trunk, Saige stood, back to the door, thin arms stirring rhythmically over a heavy-set cauldron.

"Aubree," Saige leant her ladle to one side, "I'm glad you're back. I wanted to talk to you. I know you were struggling with making the harvest. So, I've ..." She turned and took a step forward, a low table coming into view behind her. And it was then that Aubree saw.

Beneath the smoky haze, the table was cluttered with cages, bottles, knives, smears of blood. Newt's eyes in a teacup, hearts of mice half shredded on a cheese grater.

"No ..." whispered Aubree. "I set them free."

"Yes dear," Lillian touched a hand to her shoulder, "but we're witches. And pretty good at traps on top of that."

Aubree glowered at Saige. "How *could* you?"

Saige sighed, returning to stirring the cauldron. "This is a good thing. The harvest is done. You don't need to worry about it. We can all move on."

Aubree said nothing for a moment. Her eyes stung with the smoke, but she refused to blink and let the tears fall. "And what if I don't want to move on?"

Saige stopped stirring and Lillian let go of her shoulder, her normally round and rosy face taut with anxiety.

"He was only a *cat*, Aubree," said Saige impatiently.

Aubree swallowed hard, a tear running down onto her chin. She wiped it away furiously. "You just don't get it, do you?" She fought to steady her breathing, her frustration bubbling like the cauldron. "He wasn't *only* a cat. He was *my* cat. And at night he would lie next to me and in the morning he would be there. And now, *now* ..." she gasped for breath, more tears spilling down her cheeks, "now, nobody is there. And I wish *so much* I could move on, I wish it was as easy as you make out, like losing a sock or a glove. Annoying and sad but replaceable. But it's not. Because I bloody loved that bloody cat. Just like you love Lillian. So, I'm sorry, I'm SORRY if for one second all I wanted was a little less death in the world!"

Lillian pressed her hand to her mouth, eyes shining in the gloom. But Saige only groaned, swatting irritably at the low hanging herbs.

"It's not the same, Aubree. It's not the same at all! If you had died, Bramble wouldn't have *mourned* you. He wouldn't have *cried*." She turned and grabbed a handful of rat tails, throwing them into the sparking cauldron. "But you're so busy mourning *him*, you're oblivious to those who actually care about you, to those who *actually* love you."

"Bramble loved me," said Aubree defiantly.

"Oh, grow up, Aubree! Of course he didn't, he was a cat!"

Aubree took a step back, winded.

"Saige," gasped Lillian.

Saige's face fell. "Wait, I was only trying—"

But Aubree was done with listening. She turned and pushed past Lillian, shoving through the door and slamming it behind her. Marbles whinnied in welcome, but she ignored him. The ice was thickening in the cold night air, and she managed only three more steps before she plummeted onto the frozen earth, grazing her hands.

She punched the snow, eyes blurry with tears. Pathetic. That's what they thought she was, and clearly, they were right.

Bramble was a cat: of *course* he wouldn't have moped about crying at her grave like she did for him. But did that mean he didn't love her? The thought cut deep and aching. She buried her face in her skirt, breathing through the cold fabric. One more nudge of his nose, the sound of his rumbling purr. She'd give anything to have him back.

After a moment, there was a crunch of footsteps and Lillian sat down in the snow beside her.

"Have I ever told you about my first owl, Aubree?"

Aubree wiped her nose on her sleeve but didn't look up.

"I called her Sunflower, because of her wings. They were the most beautiful gold. And the gifts she'd bring me! I'd wake up with mice skittering around beneath the duvet and Sunflower perched at the foot of the bed, practically beaming with pride." She laughed, then looked down at her hands. "When Sunflower died, I told *myself* she was only an animal, that the grief wasn't so bad, because I was embarrassed. I didn't want to admit how important she was in my life. How much I really loved her."

The distant call of a pheasant drifted from the nearby woodland. "I've been a fool, Aubree," said Lillian softly. "But hearing you speak tonight, about what Bramble meant to you … I'm so sorry."

Aubree cleared her throat, her voice croaky from crying. "You heard Saige. It doesn't matter what we feel. They don't love us back."

"Do you really believe that?"

Aubree didn't reply, she just shrugged, staring down at her boots.

"You know," said Lillian, "when I first met Saige, I didn't think she even liked me, let alone that she could ever *love* me."

"But—" Aubree looked up, "you're so happy together."

Lillian laughed. "She was ever so quiet, and she never paid me any compliments or bought me flowers, or any of those silly things you sometimes dream about. But then one day she came home with a rare tea I'd been desperate to taste for years. She'd been looking for it, making private enquiries, doing everything she could to get hold of it for me."

Aubree could imagine Saige threatening local tea-dealers until they found it for her. It would've meant more to Lillian than a hundred bouquets of flowers, and Saige knew it, because she loved her. She might not show love like other people did, but that wasn't to say she didn't feel it.

"Bramble used to bring me mice," said Aubree quietly, remembering how she'd find them running around the kitchen floor, Bramble's big green eyes watching her as she scrambled after them, as if to say, "There, I knew you'd love it."

Lillian nodded, smiling. "Just like Sunflower. I suppose we all show love in different ways."

Aubree felt her breath catch as the image of Bramble faded, replaced instead by the cold, frozen night. She twisted her fingers, the grazes on her palms stinging.

"Lillian," she whispered, and Lillian looked at her. "It was my fault." She hadn't said it out loud before, and the words weighed heavy in her chest. "The cat flap froze shut. I didn't notice. He couldn't get back inside. He ... he must have been so cold."

Lillian placed a soft hand on her arm. "Opal was out that day too. I remember. It was bitterly cold. But Bramble had lived a long life. He could have sought shelter as Opal did. They say cats go away to die. And what a beautiful day to do so."

Aubree held back her tears, imagining Bramble padding out into the snow, curling up beneath a fir tree. She shook her head.

"Why did you have to ... why did you have to kill them? The animals."

"Ah." Lillian let go of her arm and clutched her hands together in the cold. "We didn't mean to hurt you. It was Saige's idea. She hated seeing you so miserable, and she really thought it would help, taking on the harvest, so you didn't have to."

Aubree looked away and Lillian fell silent.

"I just wish you'd listened to me," said Aubree eventually.

"I know. And I'm sorry. But I'm listening now. And I think Saige will listen too. She was really worried when you stormed out. And you know, listening goes both ways Aubree ..."

Aubree bit her lip. She could still feel the anger ebbing in her chest, the frustration at Saige. But Lillian was right. Saige was her friend. She had tried to do what she thought was best. She might have messed it up, but it wasn't because she wanted to hurt her. She deserved another chance, didn't she?

"Fine," croaked Aubree, wiping her nose again, then easing to her feet and brushing snow from her skirt. Her body ached from the cold, her grazed hands still stinging. She helped Lillian up too, then they both turned back towards the house. They'd taken only two steps when they saw a dark shape waiting beneath the shadow of the oak tree.

"Aubree, I—" Saige stepped forward, her usually stern face tense, her gaze fixed firmly on Aubree's boots. "I've never been very good at ... well, you know." She shuddered. "I wasn't *trying* to hurt you. The opposite in fact. But ... Misty Manor, I got caught up in it all. I just—" She glanced up at Lillian and Aubree saw how brightly her small eyes shone in the moonlight. It wasn't a warm, fuzzy kind of love. It was loyal, dedicated, proud. The kind of love that made somebody do crazy things, if only for the chance of seeing the other person smile.

"You wanted to make Lillian happy," sighed Aubree. It was obvious now.

"I suppose you're right," said Saige. "But it doesn't excuse—that is, I wanted to say … I'm sorry Aubree." She grimaced. "I'm not the best at … at *feelings.*" She cleared her throat. "But I will try. For your sake."

Aubree smiled weakly. She was exhausted. The pain of fighting, of crying. The guilt and the love. It was all so heavy. She wanted to sleep. To take a bath. To comb her hair and brush her teeth. Bramble could never come home. He could never knead her to sleep or wake up beside her, yowling for breakfast. But that didn't mean she had to be alone. That didn't mean things couldn't change for the better.

"I'm sorry too," she said quietly. "I shouldn't have assumed you'd know what I was feeling. I guess we're all a bit like Bramble in the end."

Lillian laughed and Saige let out a deep sigh. They looked at each other in the moonlight, the white drifts of snow sparkling softly around them. Then, with a small "Ah!" Saige rummaged in her dress pocket and pulled out a jar.

"I've been saving this," she said, carefully unscrewing the lid. "But I think now …"

Gradually, pure and soft, the rich song of a Phoenix slipped from the jar and curled into the night. Aubree felt a warmth fill her chest and the grazes on her palms knit gently back together.

The three witches stepped a little closer, their breaths clouding in the icy air, the warmth of the Phoenix song wrapping like a blanket around their shoulders. Then, as the song faded, Lillian grinned, her rosy cheeks bright in the moonlight.

"Did you say something about a death-free potion? Now *that* I would like to see."

•   •   •

The next day, the monthly market of the full moon hustled and bustled in the bright winter sunshine.

"Roll up, roll up!" crowed Vanessa Velentuia. "Death-free sandals, two for a pound! No! That's one for each foot, not *two pairs*, come back here!"

Aubree leaned back in her chair behind the witches' stall, inspecting the rows of bottles. The love potions were flying off the shelves. They didn't really create love of course—not even the most talented witch could do that— they only grew what was already there. Nonetheless they had sold nearly half their stock and it was only mid- morning. The death-free potions though, were completely untouched. They hadn't sold a single one, but Aubree didn't care.

"What's this then?" asked a tall female elf, picking up a bottle and peering at it. "Bramble's Fire, completely death- free ..."

"Try it." Aubree smiled.

The elf poured a little onto her palm then clapped in a shower of sparks. A beautiful phantom of a black cat flew into the air then leapt from icy puddle to snowy bank, thawing the frost.

"Hmm," she mumbled, stoppering the bottle and placing it back on the table. "I prefer the original, but I suppose these death-free alternatives never are as good as the real thing."

Aubree smiled, watching the cat leap from puddle to puddle. "I prefer the original too," she whispered.

•   •   •

Later that night, as the full moon rose over Bramble's grave, Aubree took her crochet blanket and laid it beside him under the frozen fir trees. She opened a bottle of the death-free potion and sat back in the snow, clapping her hands in a shower of sparks. She still couldn't bring herself to pluck out those five grey hairs. But as the world around her began to thaw and the phantom cats flickered through the starry sky, she whispered goodnight for the final time.

ABOUT THE AUTHOR

Rosalyn Robilliard is the pen name for two sisters living at opposite ends of England who stay in touch through writing. They love to explore new realms across fantasy, science fiction and beyond. In 2024, they were published in Volume 40 of the Writers of the Future anthology and in 2023 they won. Recently, they won First Place in the 2nd Quarter of the 2023 Writers of the Future contest, and First Place in the 2023 Mollie Savage Memorial SF&F contest.

YOU MIGHT ALSO ENJOY

POSSESSION IS NINE-TENTHS
J Dark

Possession might be 9/10th of the law. But no one mentioned 9/10th of what.

ONE FOR THE ROAD
Melissa M. Buhl & Brian C. E. Buhl

When Father Time goes missing, it's up to Tina and her best friend Alexa to use their wits and their magic to find him and bring him back.

THE JOB
Joshua Ramey-Renk

Sent to the town of Harrison to deal with threats to its livestock, Cal discovers that the thefts of the livestock are more than they seem.

Available in digital and trade paperback editions from
Water Dragon Publishing
waterdragonpublishing.com

9 781967 547784